FANGS

VAMPIRE SPY

The Fangs, Vampire Spy, series

FANGS

VAMPIRE SPY

ASSIGNMENT: ROYAL RESCUE

TOMMY DONBAVAND

WALKER
BOOKS

First published in 2013 by Walker Books Ltd
87 Vauxhall Walk, London SE11 5HJ

10 9 8 7 6 5 4 3 2 1

This book has been typeset in Helvetica and Journal

Printed and bound in Great Britain
by Clays Ltd, St Ives plc

British Library Cataloguing in Publication Data:
a catalogue record for this book is available from the British Library

ISBN 978-1-4063-3160-8

www.walker.co.uk

www.fangsvampirespy.co.uk

For Kirsty, my princess

MPI Personnel

Agent Fangs Enigma

World's greatest vampire spy

Agent Puppy Brown

Wily werewolf and Fangs's super sidekick

Phlem
Head of MP1

Miss Bile
Phlem's personal
secretary

**Professor
Hubert Cubit,
aka Cube**
Head of MP1's
technical division

Vampire spy Fangs Enigma slid back the grill from the air-conditioning vent in the ceiling and lowered himself through the gap. The steel wires attached to his body harness pulled taut and, by thumbing the buttons on the remote control in his hand, he was able to descend towards the museum exhibits below.

He tapped one of his two sharp front teeth with his tongue, causing it to light up a bright iridescent blue. "This is Fangs," he hissed. "I'm in."

From the back of an unmarked van parked outside the museum, werewolf and fellow secret agent Puppy Brown fired up the video link that would allow her to see through the camera built into Fangs's sunglasses. "Visual confirmed," she said. "I can see the crown below you."

Fangs used his remote control to lower himself a little further and then stopped. He was hanging six metres above the glass display case. "Holding position achieved," he said. "Now we wait..."

Puppy sat back in her seat. "Are you certain it'll happen tonight, boss?"

Fangs nodded to no one in particular. "According to my contact in Eindhoven, the Jade Panther will attempt to take the crown in the next hour. If we can catch him in the act, we may be able to persuade him to tell us where he's stashed the rest of his haul."

"But if we lose the crown..."

"Have a little faith, Puppy." Fangs smirked. "*I'm* on the case. What could possibly go wrong?"

Before Puppy could list her concerns, her attention was caught by a red dot flashing on the map of the museum displayed on her laptop screen. "You've got company," she hissed.

"Right on time," said Fangs, as a door at the end of the room creaked open.

A figure, dressed in dark green, crept inside and swept the beam of a powerful torch across the exhibits. It was international jewel thief the Jade Panther! Monster Protection, 1st Unit, aka MP1, had been on his trail for over a year, although no agent had so much as set eyes on him until now.

The torchlight settled on the crown and, even though the Jade Panther's face was covered with a mask, Fangs was certain the thief smiled.

The Panther produced an aerosol can and sprayed the room with what appeared to be deodorant. A matrix of red lasers appeared and the jewel thief began to manoeuvre around them carefully. A moment later, he was crouching beside the glass case containing the priceless St Edward's crown and using some sort of electronic gadget to disable the contact alarms.

With practised ease, the Jade Panther lifted the case off the crown's plinth and placed it on the floor without a sound. Then he reached for the St Edward's crown.

"Now!" cried Fangs. He flicked the "Descend" switch on his remote and plummeted towards the surprised thief – only to judder to a halt two and a half metres above him.

A new voice exploded through the blue-tooth system. It was the gurgling rasp of Phlem, the head of MP1. "This is HQ to Fangs Enigma and Puppy Brown. I have deactivated your equipment remotely. Your mission is aborted. Return to Headquarters immediately."

Fangs stared at the Jade Panther in horror. "No!" he shrieked. "You can't do that. I was just about to arrest the most wanted jewel thief in Europe."

"Do not counteract my orders, Enigma!" roared Phlem.

Fangs smashed his palm angrily against the buttons on his remote control, and a shower of sparks erupted from the motor in the air-conditioning vent above him.

Fangs spun round in a circle. The steel cables became twisted, and he dropped until he was just centimetres above the floor. He hung there like a string puppet, swinging helplessly from side to side, while the Jade Panther snatched the crown from its plinth.

"You won't get away with this, Jade Panther," Fangs snarled.

"Oh, but I will..." replied the jewel thief in a gruff voice as he tucked the St Edward's crown into his backpack. "Be seeing you." He leapt over the grid of laser beams and disappeared through the door at the end of the room.

Fangs swung helplessly in the tangle of cables, with one hand twisted behind his head and the other tied firmly to his face. Eventually, Puppy's voice broke the silence.

"Are you OK, boss?"

"I'm fine," the vampire replied. "Just feeling a little *highly strung*."

TOP SECRET

MP1 Mission File #3

Assignment: Royal Rescue

Report by: Agent Puppy Brown

I gazed out through the tinted windows of the MP1 car as the driver turned off Trafalgar Square into a side road. Beside me, Fangs Enigma was sat in silent contemplation. We'd spent most of the early morning flight back to the UK wondering why Phlem would pull us off a case at such a vital moment. One thing was for certain – if MP1 was involved, it was likely to be something weird, creepy, or both.

Our chauffeur stopped outside a garage door covered in graffiti and tapped a code into the keypad in the car's dashboard. The door opened. We drove into the small parking space beyond, and the hubbub of London disappeared as the metal entrance swung closed behind us. The wall at the back of the garage then slid away to reveal a ramp leading down into a tunnel that took us deep underground.

I glanced at my reflection in the window and smoothed down some of the fur on my cheeks. You probably know that werewolves only transform once a month, when there's a full moon in the sky. But that's not how it works with me. Something went wrong during my first transformation and I ended up permanently stuck as a wolf – apart from every full moon when I change back into a human.

There were already two or three werewolves living in my town – but unless you were with them at full moon, you never got to see them with their fur and claws. I'm the opposite. The full moon is the one night a month when I look normal. It didn't exactly make life easy.

My mum shaved me each morning before school, but by lunchtime I'd be covered in thick stubble. And my dad got weird looks from the cashiers every time he popped into the local supermarket to buy their entire stock of razors.

Thankfully, my parents' awkwardness at having a hairy daughter was short-lived as I was soon approached by MP1 – an organization that defends the world against all kinds of criminal *monster*minds. Months of secret-agent training and assignments later and here I was, gliding beneath the streets of London with my boss, Fangs Enigma – the world's greatest vampire spy (at least, that's the way he introduces himself to people).

"We're here," said Fangs, interrupting my thoughts.

We'd stopped in an underground car park,
where a trio of trumpeters greeted us with
a fanfare, and a butler stepped up to open the
car door.

"Welcome," he said, holding out a tray of
drinks. "Milk with just a drop
of blood for sir. And a freshly
squeezed orange juice for madam.
You are both expected in the blue
drawing room."

The three of us ascended several floors in
a lift and stepped out into a lavish corridor.
Fangs sipped at his drink and examined the
old-fashioned portraits in gold frames as we
walked along. "You know, this looks a lot like..."

"...Buckingham Palace," I finished, glancing
out at the courtyard through a nearby window.
"I never thought I'd get to come here."

The butler paused long enough to allow us
to peer out at the crowds taking pictures of the

Queen's Grenadier Guards in their bright-red
uniforms and black bearskin hats.

The blue drawing room turned out to be,
well ... blue. And gold. There was a lot of gold.
Waiting for us in the room was Miss Bile –
secretary to the head of MPI. She was wearing
far too much make-up for a banshee of her age.
At the sight of my boss, she
attempted to flatten down
her wild hair.

"FANGSH!" she
shrieked, her chest
heaving with
excitement and
saliva spraying
from her mouth.
"It'sh sho
good to
shee you
again."

21

"The pleasure is all mine, Bile," soothed Fangs, kissing her delicately on the cheek.

The banshee's eyes rolled back in her head and she fainted to the floor.

"Typical," gurgled a voice. Phlem, a slime beast and the head of MP1, had slithered into the room. With him was a man in his fifties who I'd never seen before. "Agents Enigma and Brown, this is Henry Catson – private secretary to Her Majesty."

At one time, a human like Mr Catson would have run away screaming at the sight of a vampire, a werewolf, a banshee and a slime beast gathered together – but that would have been before the supernatural equality laws were passed. Nowadays, meeting a zombie or a fairy was nothing to be surprised about, and I was willing to bet there were even some supernatural creatures working here at the palace.

"Please take a seat," said Catson. "I expect you're wondering why you were invited here."

"We weren't invited," said Fangs. "We were ordered to drop everything and come running."

"Don't be so melodramatic, Enigma," spat Phlem. "This is important. I take it you have heard of Princess Tiara, the queen's granddaughter?"

Fangs absent-mindedly straightened a crease in his trousers. "Is she the loud one who hires night-clubs so she can party with her posh friends, or the clumsy one who fell against the cannon during a recent twenty-one gun salute and took out an old peoples' home?"

Catson squirmed uncomfortably in his chair. "She's the, er ... clumsy one."

"Has something happened?" I asked.

Phlem nodded, making the tendrils of slime that constantly hang from his mouth wobble. "I'm afraid so, Agent Brown. Princess Tiara was opening a hospital ward in Oxford yesterday when an attempt was made to kidnap her."

Fangs, who had been about to take another sip of his drink, paused. "Attempt? You mean the kidnappers didn't succeed?"

"Thankfully not," said Henry Catson. "The princess is, you'll be pleased to hear, safe and well."

"That's good news," said Fangs, "but I still don't see what it has to do with us."

"You will when you review the CCTV footage," said Phlem.

"We'll head back to HQ and examine it immediately," I said, finishing my drink.

"No need for that, Agent Brown," Phlem said. "I have the footage here. The fewer people who know you're assigned to this case, the better."

"Assigned, sir?" said Fangs.

"Yes, Agent Enigma," said Phlem. "The princess is due to embark on a state visit to Austria tomorrow morning. You two will be her personal bodyguards."

"But we already have an assignment," Fangs protested. "Capturing the Jade Panther and retrieving the eighteen-million pounds' worth of jewellery he has stolen."

"Then consider your assignment changed," Phlem said. "Cube is waiting next door to show you the CCTV footage."

Fangs did his best to hide his sneer. "Yes, sir."

The conversation clearly over, Fangs and I made for the door. "This is ridiculous," hissed my boss. "We should be out searching for a jewel thief, not watching movies."

He opened the door, and we froze. There was a Grenadier Guard charging down the corridor towards us, his bayonet raised and bearskin hat bobbing.

"Stay back!" Fangs cried. "I'll deal with this."

After snatching a painting from the wall, Fangs raced towards the advancing soldier. The vampire waited until they were just about to

collide and then he swung the painting and hit
the guard's bearskin hat. There was a metallic

CLANG!

and the soldier's head came off and clattered to
the floor.

To my amazement, the rest of the guard
kept on running. He forced Fangs back against
the doorframe and then pressed his rifle to my
boss's throat.

"You idiot, Agent Enigma!" roared a voice.
Professor Hubert Cubit – the head of MPI's
technical division – was dashing towards us.
Cube, as he is known within the organization,
was clutching what looked like a handset
for a remote-controlled car. "I'd just finished
programming that guard – and you've
knocked out its receiver. It won't respond to any
commands now."

"It attacked me," croaked Fangs. The guard's

rifle was still pressed against his throat and it must have been difficult for Fangs to breathe.

Cube flicked a switch in the soldier's neck cavity. The guard went limp and crumpled to the ground. "He didn't attack you," Cube said. "He was running. I was using this corridor to test the mechanoid's speed."

"Mechanoid?" I asked, bending to examine the guard. He was hollow, and inside his neck, I could see wires, gears and motors. "You mean this is some kind of robot?"

"Not *some* kind, Agent Brown," replied Cube. "This is the most advanced cyborg of its type. It reacts solely to my commands and is indistinguishable from a real human being."

"Well, it wasn't reacting to your commands just then," Fangs said. "It was out of control, and I'm going to disable the other one before it does the same thing."

"Don't be ridiculous, Enigma. I was in control

the entire– Wait a minute... What other one? I've only made this prototype so far."

It was too late. My boss was already racing towards an elderly female who had appeared at the end of the corridor. She was wearing a pale yellow dress, and a crown was nestled in her sleek, grey hair.

Fangs was running straight at the queen!

"FANGS!" I bellowed. "NO!"

Fangs had grabbed the queen and was
spinning her round. "You've done a good job, Cube.
I'll give you that," he cried. "If I didn't know better,
I'd say this was a real person."

"What on earth is going on?" cried the queen.

"Don't panic," said Fangs. "I just need to rip your head off so I can reach down inside your neck and deactivate you."

By the time we reached Fangs, he had got hold of the queen's ears and was pulling with all his might. Her Majesty, however, was more than capable of looking after herself. She kicked my boss hard in the shin and then clobbered him over the head with her handbag.

Fangs hit the ground with a crash – and I hurled myself on top of him, in case he tried to get back up to have another go at removing the head of the head of state.

"I am SO sorry, Your Majesty," said Phlem as he and Henry Catson arrived on the scene at a run. "I must apologize for the actions of Agent Enigma. He's clearly lost his mind."

"It's not my fault," protested Fangs. "I thought she was a robot."

"You'll pay for this," barked Phlem. He turned back to the queen. "I shall have him removed from the assignment immediately, Ma'am."

"Nonsense," said the queen. "You shall do nothing of the sort. Misguided as he was, this vampire was trying to stop what he considered a dangerous threat. One can but hope he will act with the same eagerness while protecting my granddaughter."

"But... But..." Phlem stammered.

"No buts," insisted the queen. "If one wants one's support for MP1, one insists one give one the benefit of the doubt."

"Er ... of course, Your Majesty," Phlem said.

"With me, Catson," the queen said to her private secretary, and they both hurried away.

"Only you could get away with assaulting the queen, Enigma," Phlem said angrily.

Fangs rubbed his shin. "I don't know if I got away with it, exactly."

"Are we still on the case, sir?" I asked.

"For now," said Phlem, "but I'll be watching you very closely. MPI has only just received the queen's patronage. One step out of line and I'll have the pair of you cleaning the bottom of the Thames with toothbrushes."

At that, Phlem slithered away, leaving a trail of slime along the expensive carpet. A still-grumpy Cube led us to a nearby room.

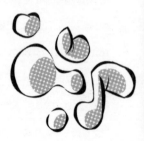

I helped the professor put the mechanoid's body on a long bench. The professor sat the robot's head on a stool and examined the damaged wiring inside. He scratched the corner of his own head pensively.

Early on in life, the professor realized that facts and information only ever come in square things. "Books, computers, filing cabinets – all square and

all filled with knowledge," he
told me during my first week
of training. "Tennis balls,
potatoes and scoops of ice
cream – all round and hardly
any knowledge in them at all."

Determined that he would
also be stuffed with information, the
young Hubert built a tight-fitting wooden box to
wear like a hat at all times, so changing the shape
of his head as it grew, from a useless sphere to a
fact-filled square. It is for this reason that he is
now known within MPl as "Cube".

"Phlem mentioned you had some CCTV footage
for us," I said.

A smile crept across Cube's face. "I can do
better than that, Agent Brown..."

He led us to a side room where there were
four video projectors, one in each corner. "By
combining the footage from four separate

33

cameras, I have been able to create a fully three-dimensional playback of the event in question."
He flicked a switch. The projectors powered up and Fangs and I suddenly found ourselves standing in a hospital forecourt, surrounded by people clutching Union Jacks. In front of us, Princess Tiara was standing by a length of red ribbon that stretched across the hospital steps.

A pretty, dark-haired young woman, wearing a nurse's uniform, was on my right. I stretched out my arm – and my paw went right through her. "She's a hologram," I gasped.

"Not quite as complex," said Cube, "although the effect is much the same."

"It's very realistic," said Fangs, looking at the attractive nurse. He whipped off his sunglasses and pulled what I've come to call his "kissy" face. "The name's Enigma," he crooned. "Fangs Enigma." He winked at the translucent beauty and then slid his sunglasses back on.

"Is there a remote we can use to control the playback?" I asked.

"No need for that." Cube smiled. Then he called out "Play!"

Instantly, the crowd around us began to wave their flags and cheer as Princess Tiara was handed a large pair of scissors.

"Pause," Cube ordered. The scene around us froze once more.

"That's incredible," I exclaimed.

"Thank you," said Cube, proudly. "I'll leave you to your work. I do, after all, have several thousand pounds' worth of mechanoid to repair." He shot a final fierce look at Fangs and then left us alone in the room.

"Ready?" I asked.

Fangs nodded.

"Play!" I shouted.

Once again the world around us began to move. The crowd cheered and the princess smiled.

"It gives me gweat pleasure to declare this glowious new hospital ward well and twuly open." She snipped through the ribbon, and the crowd applauded. The mayoress plucked a bottle of champagne from a nearby ice bucket, and a young girl scurried up the steps to hand the princess a posy of flowers. As she did so, two long lengths of bandage dropped from the hospital roof and a pair of Egyptian mummies began to abseil down them towards the princess.

The princess's bodyguard leapt in front of her, but a single blow from one mummy's massive fist sent him crashing to the ground. The other mummy snarled at the few remaining members of the crowd who hadn't run in terror and clamped a thickly bandaged hand down on Tiara's shoulder. The princess screamed.

Behind me, an engine revved noisily, and I spun round to see a third mummy driving a yellow digger across the car park at top speed. Despite knowing that this was only a video, I instinctively jumped out of the way as the vehicle pulled up to the hospital steps. The digger's bucket was lowered and the kidnappers tried to shove Princess Tiara inside.

The princess's face was forced into the bouquet of flowers she was still clutching, causing her to sneeze. *"Ah... Ah... AH ... CHOO!"* The sneeze forced her head back, where it collided with the face of the mummy behind her with a

CRUNCH!

He collapsed, clutching his broken nose to stem the flow of blood.

37

The second mummy darted forward to grab the princess, only to trip over a loose bandage and fall face first through the table on which the ice bucket was sitting. By the time he hit the ground, ice cubes were flying everywhere, and the bucket was wedged firmly over his head.

One of the ice cubes landed down the blouse of the mayoress, who screamed and dropped the champagne bottle she had been struggling to open. The bottle hit the steps, knocking out the cork. A stream of fizz sent it rocketing through the air.

It smashed through the windscreen of the digger, striking the final mummy square in the forehead and knocking him unconscious.

Distant police sirens began to wail.

"Pause!" cried Fangs.

The devastation froze around us, and we took a moment to survey the scene. A look of terror was fixed on the flickering face of Princess Tiara.

Fangs crouched down to study the mummy

with the broken nose. "The Ramses Brothers," he said. "I thought these troublemakers were in prison."

"They were released last week," Phlem said as he slithered across the room to join us. "They're back behind bars again now, but I want to know who sent them to snatch the princess."

"You don't think this was their idea?" I asked.

Fangs shook his head. "I doubt it. They tend to work as hired muscle. Tough guys, but not exactly gifted in the brain department."

"Neither are you on occasion," Phlem snarled. "But Her Majesty is insisting that I keep you on as the princess's bodyguard. Don't mess this one up, Enigma."

Fangs and I stepped onto the platform at
Innsbruck station, and stared at the royal train,
which would be our home for the next week.

"I'll say one thing for royalty," said Fangs,
removing his sunglasses to take a closer look.
"They know how to travel in style."

Princess Tiara's bags were being loaded into her private carriage by a huge man squeezed into a porter's uniform several sizes too small. Fangs and I carried our own luggage on board and then went in search of our accommodation.

As the royal security team, we had our own carriage, which included a luxurious office, complete with desks, leather sofas, Internet access and a drinks cabinet stocked with ice-cold milk for Fangs and fresh orange juice for me. (There was even a vial of A-Positive blood – his favourite flavour.) At the far end of the room were two large bedrooms with ensuite bathrooms.

"Looks like we'll be getting a little of that royal style too, boss," I commented as I sat at one of the desks and opened up my laptop. I pulled up the princess's itinerary. At that very moment – right on schedule – the train pulled away from the platform. I crossed my claws that everything else on the trip would run as smoothly.

After handing me a glass of orange juice, Fangs dropped a tiny amount of blood into his milk and then sat down on one of the plush sofas. "What's next?"

"We're due to have afternoon tea in the piano bar at four-thirty," I said.

"Afternoon tea?" said Fangs with a smile. He swung his feet up onto the sofa. "Wake me up in time to get changed..."

"This isn't a holiday," I reminded him. "We're here to protect Princess Tiara."

"From what? The Ramses Brothers are back in custody and whoever sent them won't have had the chance to put together a new plan yet. I promise you, Puppy – nothing exciting will happen this week."

Just then, the carriage door opened and Cube entered, carrying a briefcase. "I hoped I'd find you here."

Fangs sat up and groaned. "I didn't know you'd

been sent along. And I was just beginning to enjoy myself."

Ignoring the comment, Cube opened his briefcase and took out a thick metal disc with a length of thin steel cable dangling from it. "This is one of the very latest gadgets my lab has to offer."

"It's a yo-yo," said Fangs.

"Not just any yo-yo," Cube said. "It's an electric yo-yo." After winding the cable around the metal body, Cube started to spin the yo-yo up and down. "Do this ten times and you'll give the yo-yo enough charge for a single blast of electrical energy. That's enough to power a light for a few minutes, or to short out an adversary's security system. Try it."

He tossed the yo-yo to Fangs. As my boss caught it, there was a **CRACK!** that set his hair standing on end and lit both his front teeth up bright blue.

"OW!" he cried. "What in the name of Drac?"

"Oh yes," said Cube. "Be sure to discharge the yo-yo before touching it with your bare hands."

Fangs snarled and smoothed his hair back down. "I'll try to remember..."

"Any other gadgets, professor?" I asked.

"Yes, indeed," Cube replied. He pulled a packet of mints from his jacket pocket and offered one to Fangs.

"I'm not touching them," my boss cried.

"They're perfectly safe."

Fangs shook his head and tucked his hands under his cape.

"Very well," said Cube, handing the mints to me.

"What do they do?" I asked.

"They're truth mints," said Cube with a smile. "Get your suspect to eat one of these and he'll be forced to tell the truth for the next one hundred and eighty minutes."

44

"I'd best not have one, then," said Fangs.
"You might not like what I have to say about
these gadgets. Is that it? An electrical yo-yo and
anti-lying sweets?"

Cube's eyes twinkled. "I've saved the best till
last..."

And then a very strange thing happened –
all the flesh began to evaporate from Cube's body.
He was soon surrounded by a cloud of steam.

45

When the air cleared, Cube was gone! In his place was a skeleton made of metal bones and electrical wires.

"What's going on?" Fangs asked. "Who – or what – is that?"

Cube's face appeared on my laptop screen. "Impressive, isn't it?"

"Where are you?" Fangs demanded.

"Oh, I'm still at MPI Headquarters," said Cube. "You've been talking to RALF."

"RALF?" I repeated.

46

"It stands for Robotic Artificial Life Form. He's a mechanoid. I had him repaired at great expense after Agent Enigma knocked his head off at the palace."

"Wait," said Fangs. "That's the Grenadier Guard who attacked me?"

"No, RALF was what was inside the guard," Cube said from the screen. "RALF can be made to look like anyone. You just plug him into your computer or Smartphone, Puppy, and use the special software to design RALF's new look."

I stared at the robot in amazement. Cube had outdone himself this time. "How did you sneak RALF onto the train, Cube?" I asked.

"I have my ways." The professor smiled. "Why not give him a go? I've already loaded a handful of MPl personnel files into the 'demo' menu to get you started."

Following Cube's instructions, I located the socket on RALF's hip and connected the robot up

to my laptop. Then I selected a profile for him – Phlem's personal secretary Miss Bile – and clicked "Build".

Liquid bubbled out of holes in RALF's metal bones and began to take on the shape and colour of one of Miss Bile's favourite green-checked dresses. Fake skin stretched to cover the face, and grey hair sprouted out from the scalp. The eyes, ears and nose appeared – and finally the grinning mouth that we knew so well.

"Trans-for-ma-tion com-plete," announced the robot. A button lit up on the screen in front of me. "Activate personality?" I clicked on it.

The effect was astonishing. The absolute double of Miss Bile spun round to face Fangs and squealed with delight.

"Fangsh," she slobbered excitedly. "I haven't sheen you for agesh."

"It's, er ... lovely to see you too," said Fangs.

"Are you on another top-shecret asshignment?" she asked. "I've alwaysh wanted to shee the locationsh you get to vishit. You're sho lucky."

"Yes, I suppose I am..." Fangs turned to me in alarm. "Shouldn't she have fainted by now?"

I smiled. "Apparently not, boss."

The artificial banshee wiggled closer to Fangs. "Of courshe, I don't need to vishit all thoshe placesh if you bring me back shomething shpecial – like a kissh..."

My boss's brow furrowed. "A kissh?"

Miss Bile's eyes lit up. "Yesh," she spat. "A kissh." Then she lunged at Fangs, lips puckered for what promised to be the soggiest snog ever.

"Puppy!" Fangs croaked, trying to push the robotic secretary away from him. "Switch it off."

I hit the "End personality" command on my laptop and Miss Bile froze. There was a faint hissing sound and then the outer skin started to evaporate again. Two minutes later, the metal skeleton marched into a cupboard and switched itself off.

"That's amazing," I said.

"It depends on your viewpoint," said Fangs, straightening his shirt.

"Lifelike, isn't it?" said Cube from the screen. "Just try not to break him again, Agent Enigma." The screen hissed, and Cube disappeared.

"Well, I think it's all a waste of time," said Fangs. "This whole trip has been organized by one of the most security-conscious families in the world. What could possibly go wrong?"

Suddenly we heard a scream.

Fangs and I ran as fast as we could towards
the princess's accommodation, which wasn't easy
as the train had now picked up some speed and
the carriages were rocking from side to side.
We crashed through the kitchens and along the
dining carriage, dodging the waitresses who were
setting tables for dinner.

We reached the princess's carriage to find her stylist, hairdresser and make-up artist pacing nervously outside.

"What's happened?" I asked.

"We don't know," May, the princess's stylist, admitted. "The door is locked."

"We tried breaking in," said June, the make-up girl, "but we weren't strong enough."

"Stand clear," ordered Fangs. "I'll deal with this." He took a couple of steps back and then hurled himself at the door.

It didn't move.

I picked the lock with one of my claws while Fangs hopped about behind me, clutching his bruised arm and swearing under his breath. Once the door was unlocked, we told the women to wait outside and dashed into the carriage.

Princess Tiara was crouched on her bed, staring at a figure lying on the floor among shards of pottery and a handful of tulips.

52

His mouth hung open and a large, pink tongue lolled out. As Fangs flipped the man onto his back, I recognized him immediately. It was the porter who had carried the princess's bags onto the train at Innsbruck.

Taking the princess's hand, I helped her down from the bed. She was trembling. "What happened?" I asked.

"I... I'm not tewwibly sure..." she croaked. "I wanted to put some water in this vase, but when I opened the bathroom door – he was ... he was alweady inside."

Fangs took a coil of rope out of the figure's clenched fist. "It doesn't look like he was in there to wash his hands..."

"We heard you scream and came running," I said.

"Oh, that wasn't me," said the princess. "He was the one that scweamed. I pwesumed he was here to help me unpack, so I handed him the vase of

53

flowers. I didn't wealize that there was a big spider on the pot. He saw it and scweamed."

"He screamed when he saw the spider?" Fangs asked as he tied the rope around the man's wrists.

The princess nodded. "He jumped, too – and banged his head on the doorfwame before collapsing on the floor."

"OK," I said. "Once we've searched the rest of the room, we'll get him out of here, and—"

"No, you will not search my woom," the princess snapped.

"But, we need to make sure—"

"I will not have just anyone wifling thwough my pwivate possessions," Tiara insisted. "Now, take this wuffian and leave."

Tiara's assistants rushed into the room then, and so Fangs and I heaved the potential kidnapper back to our own carriage. I was almost crushed under his enormous weight. By the time we had

dropped him into an armchair, he was starting to
come round. As Fangs questioned him, I launched
MPI's facial-recognition software onto my laptop
and took his picture.

"What's your name?" Fangs asked.

The man, who was now fully awake, said
nothing. He just sat and growled at us. "GRRRRRR!"

"I said, what's your name?"

"GRRRRR!"

My laptop gave a **PING!** as a match was found
in the MPI database. I quickly accessed the file.
"Our mystery porter is called... Oh. He's called
Porter. Boz Porter. A half-giant with previous
convictions for grave-robbing and the smuggling
of stolen body parts to order."

"Trying your hand at snatching a live body for
a change, eh?" snarled Fangs. "Who sent you?"

"GRRRRRRR!"

"WHO SENT YOU?"

"He won't answer you, boss," I said.

"Oh, yes he will! Even if we have to sit here all night."

"No, I mean he can't answer you," I said. "His file says he can't speak. He's got no tongue. It was ripped out during a fight with an angry dwarf ten years ago."

"He has got a tongue," Fangs insisted. "I had to tuck it back into his mouth when I was tying him up, so he wouldn't drool all over me."

"Not according to the MPl database, he hasn't. If the file is out of date, we'll need to correct it."

Fangs turned back to the giant. "Come on, then, big fella – open up and let's have a look at this missing tongue of yours."

Porter shook his head. "Uh-uh."

"Then it's time to get firm..." Fangs said. He grabbed the briefcase Cube had given us. For a moment, I thought he was going to use one of the gadgets but, instead, he clonked the half-giant on the head with the case itself.

As Porter opened his mouth to gasp in pain, Fangs grabbed his tongue. "Got it," he cried.

And he really had got it, because the whole tongue came out in his hand.

"Yuck," exclaimed Fangs, dropping the lump of wet flesh.

I bent to examine it and noticed a small, metallic rectangle protruding from the back of it. "This is a USB connector," I said. "It plugs into a computer."

"Well, it's a whole new way of *chatting online*," said Fangs.

I picked up the tongue and plugged it into one of the USB ports of my laptop. Porter grunted and struggled against the rope tying his arms. "Whatever this is, I don't think he wants us to examine it."

"Then I guess he's going to be disappointed," said Fangs.

"It's a memory stick," I said. "And there's a video file on it."

"I always discover the best movies by *word of mouth*," Fangs quipped.

The video opened with a helicopter's view of a mansion built high up on a mountainside. Several Rolls-Royce cars were parked in the snow outside the house. Stirring classical music played as the camera swooped down over a huge outdoor swimming pool and a number of tennis courts. It zoomed in on a lone figure sitting at a table in a picturesque snowy courtyard.

The man was tall and dressed in a neat
pinstriped suit and tie. He wore a bowler hat, and
he was pouring tea into a china cup and saucer.
After adding a dribble of milk, he addressed
the camera directly. "Good day," he said. "I'm
so delighted you could join me here at the old
homestead."

There was something about him that didn't
look quite right. His skin was grey and covered
with stubble, his eyes appeared to be completely
black, and he had a scar on his chin.

He took a sip of tea and continued speaking.
"I shall be distributing this file to some of the
nastiest rotters the world has ever known and, if
you are watching it, it means you're an absolute
bounder – for which you must be congratulated."

He stood and walked through the crisp, white
snow. The camera followed him. "As you can
see, I have everything a true gentleman could

possibly desire – a beautiful home, wealth, a spiffing wardrobe, and much more. But there is something missing. I want to be married and married to someone who can offer me both power and influence. That person is Princess Tiara of the British royal family."

Fangs and I exchanged a glance.

"Now, I'm a busy man – and I don't have time to go through the whole courting ritual. So, here's my offer. I shall pay a sum of two million pounds to the first blighter to bring the princess to me here, alive and well. So, off you pop and bag me a wife! Cheerio, my fiendish friends, and good hunting."

The video ended.

"We'd better run this through the system," I said. "Phlem will want us to identify him."

"There's no need," said Fangs. "I already know who it is."

"You do?"

Fangs nodded. "His name is Barry Sasquatch. Ignore the perfect English gent act – he's a nasty piece of work."

"Sounds like you've had a run-in with him before, boss. Do you think he'll remember you?"

"I should think so," sneered Fangs. "I gave him that scar."

Princess Tiara had a few days off before her first royal engagement, and she decided to go skiing. Cameras flashed as the Austrian press surrounded her at the top of the SkiWelt ski slope.

She was immaculately dressed in a designer pink jumpsuit and goggles. Her skis, which were edged with rubies, sparkled in the bright sunshine.

Fangs and I were on the lookout for trouble. The camera on my Smartphone was linked up to the one in Fangs's sunglasses, enabling me to run every face in the crowd through the database back at MPI HQ. We were determined to find any potential kidnapper before they had a chance to act. Fangs was obviously taking the job seriously as he didn't pause too long to study the pretty, young journalist with the dark hair standing near by.

The previous evening, an unmarked MPI van had met us at Salzburg station, and a pair of security trolls had taken Boz Porter away for further questioning. I'd also handed over the half-giant's fake tongue. Cube would want to examine that back in the lab.

"... and so, I would like to thank you all vewy much for the wonderful hospitality I am enjoying in your twemendous countwy." Princess Tiara completed her speech and the photographers took their final shots, and then the ski resort's security team ushered the crowd of journalists and well-wishers away.

Tiara turned to us. "That seemed to go awfully well, wouldn't you say?"

I returned her smile. "Yes, Your Highness. Well done."

She took a deep breath. "Now, wace you to the bottom," she squeaked excitedly, grabbing her ski poles.

"Your Highness, I don't think—" my boss began, but Tiara was already gone.

It took me and Fangs a few seconds to snap on our skis, and by the time we were on the main run, the princess was little more than a pink dot in the distance.

My tinted goggles absorbed most of the glare from the snow, so I had no fear of tripping as I

crouched over my skis to pick up speed. Luckily,
the princess was travelling at a more leisurely
pace, and as Fangs and I are both expert skiers,
we were soon just a few metres behind her.

WHIP!

Out of nowhere, an arrow shot between me
and Fangs and embedded itself in the snow just
behind the princess. She yelped and shot a glance
backwards.

Three thin figures, all dressed in shimmering
white, were skiing down the slope behind us. Each
one was clutching a bow.

"Elves," Fangs hissed into his blue tooth. "They
must have hidden in the snow after the slope was
cleared. I'll hold them off – you get Tiara out of
here."

I nodded. "Your Highness!" I shouted. "Head for
the trees."

As Tiara and I sped forwards, another arrow

65

hit the snow with
a *THUD!* – and then a
third. We had to get under cover quickly.

I glanced back to see Fangs spinning Cube's
metal yo-yo – not an easy task while skiing. Once
it was fully charged, he flipped the metal disk
over the back of his hand. The yo-yo shot down its
steel cable and caught one of the pursuing elves
square in the chest. There was an electrical *CRACK!*

and a flash of light. With a scream, the elf was thrown backwards off his skis.

That just left two elves – and they were gaining fast.

Tiara and I had finally reached the forest-covered edge of the slope. As we were zigzagging between the trees, sending plumes of snow up behind us, an arrow slammed into a tree just to my right.

I turned round to see Fangs grab one of the tree branches as he passed, bending it as far as he could before ducking and letting go. The branch snapped back, catching the second elf in the face and sending him crashing into a snow bank.

The wooded area we were in was dense with foliage, and it was difficult to keep up any real speed.

WHIP!

Another arrow zipped past my ear, catching the back of the princess's right ski. She screamed and wobbled violently from side to side, but somehow managed to stay upright.

BEEP! BEEP! BEEP!

I glanced down at my phone to discover that we were heading straight for a cliff with a sheer drop of two hundred metres on the other side. We had just seconds left before we went over the edge.

"Fangs," I yelled into my blue tooth. "We're about to run out of world!"

My boss dodged to avoid the remaining elf's arrow, and then sped up to reach us. Tossing away his ski poles, he wrapped an arm around each of our waists and lifted us off the ground.

"Puppy," he shouted, "the cloak!"

I grabbed the edge of Fangs's cape as it flapped out behind us. Then I pressed a button hidden in the seam – just as we flew over the edge of the cliff. The cloak stiffened, allowing us to sail through the air.

Princess Tiara took one look at the ground far

below her ruby-studded skis and fainted, her body going limp in Fangs's arms.

My boss flashed me a wry smile.

Behind us, the third elf failed to stop and bowled over the cliff edge.

"Kind of him to *drop in*," quipped Fangs, "although I can't imagine the fall will be very good for his *elf*."

Fangs and I slumped into our seats in the dining carriage and both sighed at the same time. It was good to be sitting down.

We had landed on the outskirts of a tiny village at the foot of the mountain, and had quickly found somewhere warm and safe for the princess to rest while I called for help. Less than two hours later, we were back on board the train and on the move towards our next destination.

I glanced down to the other end of the carriage where Tiara was being served her meal. She looked a little shaken but was otherwise unhurt, and she was clearly enjoying telling the details of her adventure to her hairdresser and make-up artist, who were both listening with open mouths.

I turned back to Fangs. "Phlem sent through everything we have on Barry Sasquatch," I said, producing the handful of paperwork I had printed off. "It makes for interesting reading."

"I know everything I need to know about that villain," snarled Fangs as he added a drop of blood to his glass of cold milk. "He's trouble."

My boss wasn't wrong. The Ramses Brothers and Porter had convictions for relatively petty crimes, but Sasquatch was suspected of armed robbery, smuggling and much more. The problem was that every time he had been arrested for some wrongdoing, his team of powerful yet corrupt lawyers had sprung into action to get him acquitted, usually on a technicality.

And there was still something bothering me about his physical appearance. His head was elongated – almost retangular in shape, as though it wasn't quite human. Then it hit me.

"Barry *Sasquatch*!" I exclaimed. "*Sasquatch* is another word for a yeti. Sasquatch is a yeti, isn't he?"

Fangs nodded. "He's ashamed of it, though. He'd do anything to be accepted as human. So, he shaves himself every day and lives like a country gent."

The waitress arrived with our meals then and

I tucked my paperwork away. "Looks like we've got our work cut out."

Fangs didn't reply. He was too busy sniffing at the breast of chicken nestling beside the potatoes on his plate. "Excuse me, miss," he said, calling the server back. "This isn't *garlic* chicken, is it? Only I'm somewhat allergic to—" Then he stopped, and I realized he was staring at the waitress. She was a pretty woman with black hair. I sighed, waiting for the chat-up lines to begin...

Only they didn't.

"I've seen you somewhere before," said Fangs.

"No, I don't think so, sir," said the waitress, blushing.

"Yes, I have," Fangs insisted. "You were a nurse in the crowd when Princess Tiara opened the new ward at St Teresa's Hospital."

My boss was right! It was her.

"And you were at the press conference this morning," I cried.

Fangs grabbed the woman's arm, but she wriggled away from him and pulled a walkie-talkie from the pocket of her apron. She pressed the button on its side and screamed: "Now!"

And all the windows of the train carriage exploded inwards.

Screams rang out as five – no, six – green goblins leapt in through the broken windows, crunching over the shattered glass. Two of them made for the princess while the others jumped onto tables and snarled at anyone who dared to move.

"Here we go again," groaned Fangs, shaking glass shards off his cape. He grabbed the nearest goblin by the scruff of the neck and hurled it out of the window it had just come through. One of the others roared and darted for our table. I rammed my plate as hard as I could into its face, covering its ugly mug with mashed potato and knocking it to the floor.

We raced for the other end of the carriage – but we were too late. Two goblins had seized the princess and were already climbing out of the carriage with her, trying to muffle her screams as they went. A moment later, we heard their heavy footsteps thump on the roof above us.

"Fancy a little fresh air?" Fangs asked.

We headed for the window they had escaped out of. Claws come in extremely useful when it comes to climbing sheer surfaces. The goblins had used theirs to cling to the outside of the train carriage and climb up onto the roof – and

I followed suit, with my boss slotting his fingertips into the holes I made with my sharp talons.

The train was rocking from side to side, making it difficult to maintain our balance – but we knew we had to keep going. In the fading light, we could just make out that the goblins were dragging the princess onto the roof of the next carriage.

My sensitive werewolf ears picked up the faint

WUMPH! WUMPH! **WUMPH!**

of distant rotor blades – and the sound was getting louder. "They've got a helicopter coming, boss. We'll have to—"

Fangs pushed me face down onto the carriage roof – just as we passed under a low stone bridge. That was close! A split-second later and the top half of me would have been rolling along at the side of the track.

The helicopter swooped low over our heads, coming to a stop over the two goblins holding the princess. A rope ladder was thrown out and one of the goblins caught it with gnarled claws.

We dashed along the top of the carriage towards them. I landed on top of Princess Tiara, making her yelp. The two furious goblins turned on us, swinging out with their claws. My boss managed to block the first three swipes, but the fourth caught him off-guard and

he fell backwards. One goblin
hurled itself on top of
him and the pair
wrestled,
rolling over
and over,
until they
fell into
the gap
between the
carriages.

"Fangs!" I yelled.

78

As I was distracted, the remaining goblin – the one holding the helicopter's ladder – made a grab for the princess. I sank my teeth into his leg. He let go of the rope ladder and twisted round to hit me – but I was quicker. I pulled his foot out from underneath him. He crashed down onto the roof and bounced off the train into a clump of trees.

At that moment, the helicopter banked hard left and disappeared into the evening sky behind us. That just left the three goblins inside the train and the one that had pushed Fangs down between the carriages.

My boss was scrambling back onto the roof of the train. The goblin who had attacked him was nowhere to be seen.

"Are you OK?" I asked.

Fangs nodded. "Lucky we're trained for this sort of stuff."

"And your friend?"

"He's on the right *track* now..."

Between us, we managed to lift a shaking Tiara down from the roof and help her back inside the train. The other three goblins were nowhere to be seen, but we found the princess's assistants curled up beneath one of the tables.

"Where did they go?" Fangs asked.

"D-down that way," said April, pointing in the direction of our carriage. "They took the waitress with them."

"I'm pretty sure she wasn't a real waitress," I said.

We left the princess in the care of her

assistants and set off in search of the remaining
would-be kidnappers.

The goblins had left a trail of destruction
and a load of terrified train staff behind them.
The kitchens were trashed, the piano bar
ransacked and someone had drawn a moustache
on a portrait of the queen in the games room.
We reached our carriage and paused outside.

"On three," Fangs whispered to me. "One, two,
three."

We burst in through the door together – but
the carriage was empty. And I mean *empty*. The
goblins and whoever the dark-haired girl was
had taken all of our important MPI equipment:
my laptop, Cube's briefcase – and RALF the
robot skeleton. This must have been where the
helicopter had gone after it had left us on top
of the train.

I slumped into an armchair. "Cube won't be
happy that we lost RALF," I said.

"Cube can go and boil his square head," scoffed Fangs. "We saved the princess – again. That's what we're here for – not to protect his precious toys."

"You know these attempts to kidnap her are going to continue until we get to Sasquatch, don't you?"

Fangs pulled open the drinks cabinet and filled a glass with milk before adding a healthy splash of A-Positive. "We don't know where he is, though. The only way we'd find him would be to *allow* the princess to be taken." His eyes widened as the idea sank in.

"We can't allow Tiara to be kidnapped."

"Of course not," said Fangs. "But what if the next lot of attackers thought they'd got her...?"

"You mean let them kidnap someone disguised as the princess?"

Fangs nodded. "Someone with MP1 training who was just playing the part. They'd lead us right to Sasquatch."

82

"That's brilliant, boss," I said. "But who'll pose as Tiara? We've lost RALF now and I'm far too hairy."

Fangs took a sip of his drink. "Well, if you can't do it, then who can?"

Fangs stood before the class of Austrian primary-school children and tried to smile without revealing his sharp teeth. The princess's assistants had done a wonderful job. He looked gorgeous. May, the stylist, had adjusted one of

Tiara's designer pink dresses so that it fitted Fangs snugly, and June had worked wonders with his make-up. You really couldn't see his pale flesh or the dark rings around his eyes – his cheeks blossomed with pink blusher, and a pale red lipgloss really brought his lips to life.

April, Princess Tiara's hairdresser, had been given the toughest job. She'd had to make a wig that matched the princess's hair from the spare extensions she had in her kit. There wasn't quite enough fake hair to completely cover Fangs's jet-black locks, so she had attached the extensions to the inside of one of Tiara's summer hats. So long as Fangs kept the bonnet in place, no one would be any the wiser.

It's fair to say that Fangs hadn't exactly been thrilled about standing in for Princess Tiara – but allowing a body double to be kidnapped in the princess's place was his idea, and it was the only way we could think of to get to Sasquatch.

Of course, we'd had to run the plan past HQ. Cube had been too furious about his robot being stolen to pay much attention, but everyone else in London had thought the plan brilliant. In fact, they'd insisted I take photographs of Fangs in the disguise to bring back to HQ.

Now my boss was at the front of the classroom, trying to look both regal and feminine. The real Princess Tiara was posing as a junior secretary. She was standing at the back of the room with April, May, June and me.

The teacher gave a speech to welcome their most-esteemed visitor, and then surprised us all by handing Fangs a book and asking if it would be possible for the princess to read the children a story. "It would greatly help their learning of English," she explained.

Fangs threw me a worried glance – we'd worked on the assumption that the kidnapping would take place before he would have to speak.

Unfortunately – despite conducting a thorough search of the school grounds on the way in – we hadn't found a single supernatural character.

Fangs took the book and sat on a tiny chair.

"Ahem," he said, clearing his throat in an effort to keep his voice high-pitched. "Hello, kiddies." He swallowed nervously. "I'm very happy to be here today…"

I coughed loudly. "Are you very happy, or VEWY happy, Your Highness?" My boss had forgotten to impersonate the princess's habit of mispronouncing the letter "R".

"Of course," said Fangs. "I'm, er … VEWY happy to be here in Austwia, and especially to be visiting your classwoom on behalf of the Bwitish woyal family."

The teacher led the children in a polite round of applause.

"Now," said Fangs, starting to get the hang of the voice. "Let's all enjoy a stowy together,

87

shall we?" He opened the book and sighed. It was *The Incredible Perils of Roger the Red Rabbit*. This was going to be tough.

"*Woger, the wed wabbit, was getting weady for the big wunning wace on Fwiday,*" Fangs began.

Suddenly, one of the children began to growl. Then another child – a cute young girl in pigtails – joined in. Then a boy with short, spiky hair started growling too. Before long, the whole class

of five-year-olds was snarling like wild animals.

I glanced over at the teacher, but she remained stony faced. And now I looked more closely at her, she seemed to be somehow familiar...

It was the dark-haired waitress from the train!

And the growling children weren't children at all – they were pixies! We'd walked right into a trap. "Oh no!" I shouted. "We have to get Princess Tiara out of here at once." We had agreed that we'd have to put up a fight when the attack came, or the kidnappers would suspect that something was wrong. I waded through the pixies, trying to reach Fangs.

I was too late. The teacher produced a large sack from her desk drawer and pulled it over Fangs's head. He gave me a sly wink as he disappeared inside the bag.

Believing they had the princess trapped, the pixies turned on the rest of us. We pretended to be terrified (although I don't think much acting was required in Tiara's case), and we backed away as the teacher dragged Fangs out into the playground and then into a waiting car. The tyres squealed as the vehicle sped away, taking my boss with it.

Their task complete, the pixies sneered at us one last time, then raced for a bookcase at one end of the room. They shoved it aside to reveal a hole smashed into the wall and – one by one – they disappeared through it. Finally, the room fell silent.

"Is that it?" squeaked Tiara. "Am I safe now?"

"For the time being," I assured her.

"But what about when the kidnapper meets Fangs?" asked June. "Our disguise was pretty good, but it won't fool anyone who looks too closely."

"I'll be there long before anyone gets a good look at him," I said. "Now, you three take Princess Tiara back to the train and stay there until you hear from me. I've arranged for the local security trolls to look after you."

* * *

I revved the engine of my sports car and pulled out into the traffic. Luckily, MP1 keeps cars parked in key locations of all major cities and all I'd had to do was press my thumbprint against the lock to gain access. I clipped my Smartphone

into the dock on the dashboard and activated the GPS app. The software wasn't as powerful as the one on my laptop, but as that had been stolen, this was all I had.

PING!

A red dot began to flash on the map displayed on the screen of my phone. Excellent! The tracking device April had sewn into Fangs's padded bra was working perfectly. I set off in pursuit.

* * *

The journey to Sasquatch's estate took a little over two hours. I quickly caught up with the kidnappers' car and settled back to follow at a discreet distance. Then I tapped my blue tooth and made a call to update Phlem on the situation. I could hear Cube in the background, still ranting about the loss of his robot – but I wasn't in the mood to argue and so, as soon as I'd given my report, I ended the call.

The kidnappers' car pulled off the main road just as we reached the city of Graz and I pulled over to give them a head start. It had been easy enough to hang back and mingle with the traffic on a busy motorway, but they were bound to spot me if I followed too closely down a country lane. Besides, the GPS software would tell me exactly where Fangs was.

I drove along the back road for a few miles until I found myself approaching the same luxurious mansion I had seen in Sasquatch's video. Abandoning the car, I completed the journey on foot. Once at the house, I skirted around the back to try and find a way inside. It wasn't easy. Guards in black jumpsuits were on patrol in the grounds, and some of them had dogs.

Finally, I found an open window and slipped inside. The interior was as sumptuous as the exterior. Every room was filled with priceless works of art and expensive antiques. I forced myself to concentrate on finding Fangs and tracked the red dot on my phone until, eventually, I heard voices coming from a nearby room.

The door was slightly ajar, and I peered through the crack to see the dark-haired girl push Fangs into a chair at one end of a long dining table. The sack was still over his head. "Oh my," he said, keeping up the charade of being the princess. "This is vewy distwessing."

The girl tied Fangs's wrists to the back of the chair and smiled. "It'll all be over soon," she promised. Then, certain her captive couldn't escape, she disappeared through a side door.

I hurried into the room and crouched down behind Fangs's chair, as I worked to untie his hands.

"I do wish you'd make up your mind," said Fangs in his best Tiara voice. "Either you want the wope tied awound me, or you don't."

I pulled the sack off my boss's head. "It's me," I hissed. "The plan worked."

Fangs sighed and pulled the hat and fake hair off his head. "Let's find Sasquatch and put an end to this."

"That might not be easy," I said. "This place is huge."

"Oh, I don't think it will be that difficult, my dear," said a familiar voice.

The chair at the other end of the dining table swivelled round to face us. Sitting in it, stroking a fluffy white sheep, was Barry Sasquatch.

"Fangs Enigma," he sneered. "We meet again."

Fangs sneered back at the villainous yeti.

"Sasquatch," he growled. "You recognize me, then?"

The corners of Sasquatch's mouth twisted into what may have been a smile. "As much as you would like to think that your impersonation of Princess Tiara is a flawless success – I am not fooled by it, and neither was my assistant."

Fangs raised an eyebrow. "Assistant?"

The pretty, young woman with jet-black hair came back into the room.

"Allow me to introduce Miss Issy Death," said the yeti, stroking his sheep.

"We've already met," said Fangs. "Several times."

"Ah, yes... Miss Death has been overseeing the kidnap attempts. One simply can't trust hired henchmen to complete an assignment these days. And, of course, you now have an assistant yourself." He turned to me. "Welcome, Miss Brown."

I jumped at the sound of my name. I'd spent the last minute or so tapping my blue tooth with my tongue and trying to get an update back to HQ.

"I'm afraid your blue tooth won't work here, Miss Brown," Sasquatch explained. "I use specialist radio equipment to block all unwanted communication in and out of my home, but I hope this will not adversely affect your stay with us."

97

"Stay?" I asked. "What makes you think we're staying?"

"Oh, come now," said Sasquatch, pretending to sulk. "Surely you'll both stay for dinner, at the very least. I insist..." He flicked a glance at the window, beyond which three of his guards were standing, each clutching a rifle.

"I guess we're staying for dinner," I said.

"Excellent," Sasquatch said. "Minty will be delighted to have company."

I looked around the room. "Minty?"

"This is Minty," Sasquatch explained, tickling the sheep under the chin. It let out a satisfied "BAAA!"

"He used to have a cat," said Fangs, "but it was too small and looked ridiculous in his gigantic yeti hands."

Sasquatch's face twisted with rage. "Do not use that disgusting word around me."

"Which word?" Fangs asked innocently. "Yeti?"

98

"Stop it! You won't win this time, Enigma. It is I who shall emerge from this encounter victorious."

"That would certainly make a change." Fangs smiled.

"Silence!" Sasquatch looked as though he was about to explode. "Issy, bring in our special guest."

Issy Death disappeared into the back room again. When she re-emerged, she wasn't alone. I gasped. April and May – two of the royal assistants – were holding Princess Tiara by the arms.

"What's going on?" Fangs demanded.

I glared at April and May. "You were supposed to be protecting her."

Sasquatch was smiling again. "Please, Mr Enigma, do calm yourself. To answer your question, Miss Brown – these young ladies work for the highest bidder... Me. As do the two security trolls you sent to guard the train."

"And June?" I asked. "What have you done with her?"

"Oh, she's one of us as well." April smirked. "She's busy packing up Her Royal Wetness's belongings and will be here later."

Princess Tiara struggled to free herself from the grip of her former assistants. "Leave my pwoperty alone! I will not have it wummaged thwough."

"Oh, do give it a rest." Sasquatch sighed. "You're giving me a headache."

"No, I will not give it a west," shrieked Tiara. "I have been bwought here against my will, and I demand you welease me immediately."

Sasquatch ignored her and spoke directly to Issy. "Take her to her room and make sure she's locked inside it."

Issy nodded and led the trio away. We could hear the princess complaining loudly as she was dragged deeper into the house.

"Not exactly the way I would have expected you to speak to your future bride," said Fangs.

"Bride?!" Sasquatch laughed as he poured himself a glass of wine. "What makes you think I'm going to marry her?"

My boss and I exchanged a glance. "The video you made and sent out to every lowlife and thug known to man," I said.

Sasquatch appeared genuinely surprised. "Oh, you've seen that? Good, wasn't it? I thought I came across rather well." He paused to stroke Minty the sheep. "I had to give those scoundrels a reason for my wanting the princess – but there's no way I'll be taking her hand in marriage. Could you imagine a life with *her*?"

"Then why do you want her?" Fangs asked.

"Why, to return her to her family, of course."

I was starting to get a bit of a headache. "Wait – you're offering two million pounds for someone to kidnap Princess Tiara, just so you can take her back?"

"It's as simple as that," said Sasquatch.

101

"Although I would *expect* to receive some form of reward for her safe return, of course."

"Of course," said Fangs. "Your two-million pounds' investment back, plus a generous bonus, I presume?"

"Oh, nothing so crude as money," said Sasquatch with a scowl. "No, I will insist on receiving a royal castle for my trouble! Windsor Castle, preferably. And imagine my luck at being able to disgrace my old rival, Fangs Enigma, into the bargain. The secret agent who couldn't even look after a pesky princess."

Fangs fixed Sasquatch with a hard stare. "That's not going to happen."

"And why not?"

"Because I intend to stop you and return Princess Tiara to the palace myself."

Sasquatch began to chuckle. His laughter grew louder and louder, and even Minty the sheep seemed to join in with a hearty "BAAA!"

Fangs was unperturbed. "I never did tell you how I gave him that scar, did I, Puppy?"

Sasquatch stopped laughing.

"It's the most ridiculous story," continued Fangs. "You see – this isn't Sasquatch's first attempt at being accepted into polite society. Years ago he managed to wangle an invite to a political fundraiser at London Zoo, hosted by none other than the prime minister, Sir Hugh Jands."

"I'm warning you, Enigma..."

Fangs ignored the threat. "I was on the security team that night, and it was my good fortune to tell old Barry here that his invite was a fake and that I wasn't going to let him in. But our friendly neighbourhood yeti wasn't going to let something as small as a counterfeit invitation stop him from mixing with the gentry. So he went round to the back of the zoo and climbed over the wall..."

I couldn't help but smile. "What happened?"

"He climbed straight into the children's petting zoo and was attacked by a family of angry guinea pigs. By the time I heard his screams and dragged him out, he was bleeding and had a deep wound on his cheek."

"ENOUGH!"

Sasquatch leapt to his feet, knocking Minty the sheep to the floor and overturning his chair. "You will rue the day that you ridiculed me, Fangs Enigma. I am more human than you will ever be! And when I have moved into my royal castle, I will never have to associate with you disgusting supernatural creatures again."

Fangs thought for a second and then smiled. "So, what you're saying is ... you ain't seen nothin' *yeti*."

Fangs and I were led upstairs and locked inside adjacent rooms with the order to be ready for dinner at seven-thirty p.m. My room was extremely lavish with an ensuite bathroom and a wardrobe full of beautiful dresses. I presumed my boss was enjoying a similar level of hospitality.

Sasquatch had stormed out of the room after Fangs had finished his story, ending our earlier meeting with a flurry of insults. My boss really knew how to touch a nerve with this guy, and I hoped he wouldn't be tempted to push him a little too far.

At exactly seven-thirty, our rooms were unlocked and a different pair of guards ushered us back downstairs to the dining room. We were both dressed to the nines: Fangs in an expensive dinner suit and me in a designer dress.

"Barry makes his apologies," Issy said as we arrived. "He has a little business to attend to, and is running late."

"This is our chance," Fangs whispered. "Watch the door while I use a truth mint on Miss Death."

I took up my position near the piano where one of Sasquatch's guards was picking out a melody.

Fangs sauntered over to Issy. "May I join you for a drink?" he asked, gesturing to the milk.

"But, of course..." Sasquatch's assistant poured a second glass of milk and the pair made their way to the dining table. Fangs stood behind Issy and emptied a crushed truth mint into his drink.

"What an incredible evening," he crooned, taking a seat. "Chilled milk, beautiful company, and such wonderful scenery..." He glanced out of the window. "Just look at the way the floodlights glint off the perfect white snow."

As Issy turned to admire the view, Fangs quickly switched the drinks round so that his glass – the one with the truth drug – was nearest her.

"One of us should propose a toast," said Issy, turning back to flutter her eyelashes at Fangs.

"To us..." My boss raised his glass and clinked it against Issy's – a little too hard. The milk spilled down the back of her hand.

"Oh my," she said. "Do you think you could pass me a napkin?"

"Of course," said Fangs, setting his glass down. As soon as his back was turned, Issy switched the drinks again.

"Now, where were we?" she asked.

Fangs picked up the glass closest to him – the one containing the truth mint – and smiled. "I was gazing into your eyes and making a toast."

"Of course..."

I coughed. Loudly. Fangs looked over to me, confused. All I could do was snatch up two empty glasses from the piano and mime switching them round. His eyes widened in acknowledgement and he said, "Is it me or does the pianist look familiar?"

Issy looked at the piano player, giving Fangs just enough time to switch the drinks back again. "Of course," she said, turning back. "He's one of Barry's–" She stared suspiciously at the two glasses.

"Oh, look," she said, gesturing to the kitchen. "I think our meals are coming."

"They shouldn't be ready yet," said Fangs, checking his watch. "I thought we were waiting for—" He looked at the table. As Issy was switching the drinks, she had accidentally knocked the

glasses together and milk was sloshing onto the tablecloth.

It was Fangs's turn to make a move. "Monkey with a lightsabre!" he yelled, pointing over Issy's shoulder. She spun round in fright, giving Fangs the chance to swap the drinks one more time. The table was now soaked in spilled milk.

I sighed.

The pair stared at the mess. It was clear that neither of them was able to tell which drink was which. So, Fangs went to Plan B and pulled out the packet. "Mint?"

"What are those?" demanded a gruff voice. I'd been too busy watching Fangs and Issy to spot Sasquatch on his way down the stairs.

"Nothing," said Fangs innocently. "Just mints." He took a deep breath and popped one of them into his mouth to demonstrate.

"Well, don't spoil your dinner," said Sasquatch, calling for one of his guards to clean up the spilled milk. "Please take your seats."

Fangs finished the mint as we took our places at the table. Then the guards who had brought us down from our rooms reappeared with Princess Tiara. She looked very grumpy as she took the last-remaining seat.

"Well," said Sasquatch. "Isn't this nice...?"

The door to the kitchen quarters opened and several of the yeti's guards entered carrying the first course. They locked the door behind them. With further guards now stationed at the other entrances to the dining room, there was no way out.

111

"So, tell me Miss Brown..." Sasquatch asked as we ate. "How did you get involved with MP1 and my old adversary?"

Before I could reply, Fangs said something none of us expected to hear. "I've got an itchy bum."

We all sat in stunned silence for a moment – and then it hit me. The truth mint had kicked in.

"I'm ... er ... very sorry to hear that, Mr Enigma," said Issy.

"You've got pretty lips," Fangs said to her. "I'd like to kiss you." Then to Sasquatch: "I don't want to kiss you."

Sasquatch cleared his throat. "I'm very glad to hear it." He addressed the princess. "And how is your meal, Your Highness?"

"I wore her knickers today," Fangs blurted out before the princess could reply.

Sasquatch stared at him. "What?"

"I once wore a pink tutu, as well," Fangs said. "I took ballet lessons until I was eighteen."

"Mr Enigma, what do you think you are doing?" Sasquatch asked.

"I'm doing what I always do," said Fangs. "I'm thinking about penguins."

Then the door burst open and June – the princess's former make-up artist – barged in, a bag clutched in her hand. I could barely look at her knowing how she'd betrayed Tiara.

"What do you want?" Sasquatch asked. "I gave you strict instructions that we were not to be disturbed."

"I know that," replied June. "But I wanted to tell you that I've brought the princess's belongings here and unpacked them, as ordered."

"And...?"

"And I found something very interesting in a secret compartment in one of her suitcases."

The princess groaned as June reached into the bag and pulled out a purple-and-gold crown that was studded with over 400 precious stones.

I thought I was seeing things. "The St Edward's crown," I croaked. "The one stolen from the Rijksmuseum in Amsterdam."

Sasquatch was staring at the crown. He was as stunned as the rest of us.

"There were also these," said June, tossing a matching dark-green balaclava and pair of gloves onto the table.

"But that must mean—" I said.

"Yes," snapped Princess Tiara, jumping up. "I'm the Jade Panther! And that crown belongs to me."

In one swift movement, she spun round and kicked June in the chest, sending her crashing to the ground. One of Sasquatch's guards immediately rushed over, but he was quickly dispatched with a karate chop to the back of the neck.

Before the guards had time to react, Tiara sprang up onto the table and grabbed the priceless crown. "Now, if you'll excuse me, I'll be leaving," she spat. She ran the length of the table, somersaulted onto the piano and cartwheeled towards the door – just as six of Sasquatch's men reached her. She took two of them out with a single roundhouse kick, but she was unable to fight them all off. It took five guards to hold her still and the sixth gave the crown to his boss.

Fangs was the first to comment on the sudden change in Tiara's personality. "Your voice is different," he said. "What happened to all that 'woyal twip' stuff?"

Tiara sneered. "You mean the 'fwagile pwincess' act?" she said, reverting to the twee voice we'd come to know. "That's just for the public. I hate the royal life and would do anything to leave it behind. I can look after myself."

Sasquatch stood and then made his way across the room to stand before the princess. "You most certainly can, my dear," he soothed. "And now that I know your secret identity, I'm beginning to wonder whether I've been too hasty in my decision not to marry you."

Princess Tiara gazed up at Sasquatch, her eyes twinkling. "Well, you have put in an awful lot of effort to get me here. What can you offer?"

Sasquatch smiled. "A life of crime – together. Imagine what we could steal if we combined your skills and my resources. We'd be unstoppable."

Then, suddenly, they were kissing. Not just a quick peck, mind – a full-on snog. I buried my face in my paws. Surely this evening couldn't get any worse!

"I need a wee-wee," said Fangs.

I woke up with a start and, for a second, couldn't remember where I was. Then it all came flooding back. Barry Sasquatch... Princess Tiara... Fangs and the truth mint...

He had moaned all the way to bed the previous night that he didn't think he'd be able to get to sleep without his teddy bear, Mr Tinkle-Pants.

118

I was just making a mental note to ask Cube to make an antidote to the truth mints for future use when the door opened and Fangs entered.

"I didn't know the doors were unlocked," I said.

"I think Sasquatch must be in a good mood," said Fangs. "Have you looked outside yet?"

I jumped out of bed. The scene that greeted me in the courtyard below my window made my jaw drop. Dozens of Sasquatch's guards were setting out rows of chairs while others busied themselves by erecting a white silk awning and filling any empty space with flower arrangements.

"They're doing it," I gasped. "They're getting married! I have to find the princess and talk to her."

Fangs grabbed my arm. "There's no point, Puppy."

I stared at my boss in surprise. "What?"

"Let's just get out of here," he said. "Tiara's happy where she is."

119

"We can't just leave... We're supposed to protect her – even if she decides to make a terrible mistake. Plus, she's the Jade Panther! She should be put under arrest and then interrogated to find out about the rest of the stuff she stole. The missing crown may be here, but that leaves eighteen-million pounds' worth in other jewellery still missing."

Fangs shrugged. "Arresting the princess wouldn't exactly be protecting her. I say we head back to HQ and tell Phlemington we failed in both assignments."

My eyes narrowed. "Tell *who* we failed?"

Fangs paused for a second. "Phlem."

"That's not what you said. You said 'Phlemington'."

"No, I didn't."

"Yes, you did."

"Well, it's his full name," protested Fangs. "At least it is according to his MPl personnel file."

Now I knew something was wrong. "When did you read Phlem's file?"

"It was on your laptop."

"I don't have MP1 personnel files on my laptop," I said.

"Yes, you do," Fangs insisted. "Cube sent them to you to test out the software for his mechanoid."

"But we only accessed Miss Bile's file, and then my laptop was stolen by the goblins..."

"Never mind that now," said Fangs. "Get your stuff together and we'll meet downstairs."

"Sorry, boss," I said, "that's a 'no'. And if you really *are* my boss, then I'm also sorry for this..."

I opened my jaws wide and sank my teeth into Fangs's arm. I immediately knew I was right! I was biting into metal.

"You're RALF!" I cried, pulling my Smartphone from my belt.

The robotic Fangs growled at me. "What are you going to do with that? All communication is blocked. You can't call for help."

"No, but I can use the app Cube sent me to deactivate you." I prodded at an icon with my  claw and the figure before me began to dissolve, melting away until all that was left was the silver skeleton. Once I was sure RALF was no longer a threat, I went in search of the real Fangs.

I found him bound and gagged in his bathroom. "We have to hurry," I said as I untied him. "Sasquatch and Tiara are about to get married."

I showed him the scene in the courtyard below.

Everything was now set up. The band was tuning its instruments and guests were beginning to arrive. Sasquatch must have invited them all late the previous night – and he can only have used the address book marked "Undesirables", as everyone there was a supernatural criminal of some kind.

"There are the goblins we fought on top of the train," said Fangs. "Or a few of them, at least. The others must still be in hospital."

"And there," I said, pointing, "are the elves that attacked us on the ski slope."

"We have to find Princess Tiara and get her out of here," said Fangs. "She may be a jewel thief, but we can't let her sink so low as to mix with this sort of crowd."

"Let's split up," I suggested. "We'll work more quickly that way."

We burst out of the room and ran in opposite directions along the corridor.

The first two rooms I searched were empty, but I could tell that the third was in use. The bed had been slept in, and the shower was running in the bathroom. Suddenly, the door to the ensuite swung open and Sasquatch emerged. I threw myself under the bed and held my breath.

He sat at the dressing table and began plucking his bushy eyebrows with a pair of salad tongs. Luckily, he hadn't seen me – but I couldn't think how I was going to get out of there.

Then I spotted that the door to the corridor was still ajar. If I could crawl behind the yeti without making a sound, I might just be able to escape...

Slowly, I slipped out from beneath the bed and began to crawl. So long as I managed to stay quiet... Then, as I was inching forwards, Sasquatch dropped the salad tongs. They bounced on the carpet and landed on the floor, just inches from my paw. I froze.

A huge, grey hand began to feel about for them. Sasquatch's fingers touched my wrist and then he ran his fingers over the fur on my arm. I'd had it now – unless...

"BAAA!"

It wasn't the best sheep impression in the world, but it seemed to do the trick as Sasquatch patted me on the head and said, "Good girl, Minty!" Then after grabbing the tongs, he went back into the bathroom and closed the door behind him. I don't think my heart started again until I was outside in the corridor.

I searched the rest of that floor but found no sign of the princess. Just as I heard the band outside begin to play the bridal march, I came across a room with no furniture in it at all – just a huge yellow hang-glider and two matching yellow helmets. It seemed an odd place to keep sports equipment, but I didn't have time to consider it further. I had to get downstairs. The wedding ceremony was about to start.

I raced back into the corridor – straight into the clutches of one of Sasquatch's armed guards.

Sasquatch's guards had already captured Fangs, and they made a big deal of marching us both out into the courtyard. By the time we got there, Tiara was walking down the aisle. Despite the rushed arrangements, she looked stunning in her white silk dress – and instead of a bouquet of flowers, she was holding the St Edward's crown. Sasquatch

also looked the part in a designer suit and top hat,
and even Minty the sheep had been treated to a
pink ribbon around her neck.

The guards stood us at the back of the seating
area while the ceremony took place. We waited
quietly until the registrar – an elderly fairy with
bullet holes in one of her wings – said, "Does
anyone here have any just cause or reason why
these two should not be joined in marriage?"

Fangs sprang into action. "Yes!" he yelled,
head-butting the guard behind him and
snatching his rifle. "I have something to say."
For one horrible moment, I thought Fangs was
planning to use the gun on Sasquatch, but I
needn't have worried. He snapped the rifle over
his knee, tossed the bulk of the weapon away and
then popped a mint inside the barrel. He blew
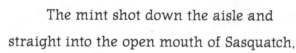
down the barrel as hard as he could.

The mint shot down the aisle and
straight into the open mouth of Sasquatch,

who was demanding his guards stop Fangs.
He gagged and then swallowed.

"Hey, Sasquatch – why don't you tell your
guests why you really asked them to kidnap
Princess Tiara?" Fangs shouted as a guard
grabbed him.

"You know full well that I want to be made a
lord so I can stop associating with these freaks,"
Sasquatch growled. Then his eyes widened in
terror as he realized what he'd just said, and he
clamped a hand over his mouth.

The truth mint was working! Several of the
guests were beginning to sit forward in their
chairs, and they did not look happy.

"But I thought these people were your friends,"
Fangs said.

"Friends?!" spat Sasquatch. "I hoped as many of
them as possible would be caught while trying to
kidnap the princess."

The crowd looked angrier.

"Ah yes," said Fangs. "The princess! What have you learned about her?"

Sasquatch clenched his teeth together, but the sound still came out. "She's the Jade Panther," he growled. "She's stolen eighteen-million pounds' worth of precious gems, and only she knows where it's all hidden."

You could almost see the wave of greed wash over the faces of the assembled villains.

"And, finally," yelled Fangs, "when you are the owner of a royal castle, what do you plan to do with freaks like us?"

Sasquatch couldn't help himself. "If I get my way, you'll all be locked up or exterminated for the scum you are."

The furious crowd had heard enough. They surged towards Sasquatch and his bride-to-be. The guards tried to fight their way to their boss, but there were just too many angry creatures in the way.

The courtyard descended into chaos as the

supernatural villains began to turn on one another. A pair of ogres tore down the marquee, the zombies lashed out at the elves, and the goblins began beating one another over the head with unopened wedding gifts.

Meanwhile, Sasquatch and Tiara were running hand in hand through a side door into the house.

"Come on!" I yelled to Fangs.

We fought our way through the angry mob, half of them livid at Sasquatch's plans to have them exterminated like bugs. Others set about ransacking the mansion in search of the Jade Panther's stolen haul.

Fangs and I followed Sasquatch and Princess Tiara up the marble staircase and along the corridor to the room containing the hang-glider. Issy Death was waiting with the yellow helmets. After handing them to Sasquatch and Tiara – who were already in the hang-glider harnesses – she slammed her palm against a button beside the

light switch, and the entire back wall and part
of the floor fell away, opening the house directly
onto a sheer drop that led down the snowy
mountainside. Fangs and I were forced to jump
back for our own safety.

Issy was just starting to clamber onto the
hang-glider behind Sasquatch and Tiara (who was
still clutching the St Edward's crown) when—

"BAAA!"

"Minty!" cried Sasquatch. His pet sheep came
running into the room at top speed, leapt over the
gap in the floor and landed in Issy's harness.

"Get out of there, you disgusting animal!" Issy
screamed, giving Minty a sharp smack across
the behind.

"BAAAAAAAA!"

"Nobody treats my Minty like that," the yeti
roared. He hurled Issy across the room. She

collided with Fangs and me, sending us crashing
onto what was left of the floor.

By the time we were back on our feet,
Sasquatch, Tiara and Minty were flying across
the snowy valley below.

They had got away.

CASE UNRESOLVED

SIGNED: Agent Puppy Brown

Princess Tiara stepped up to the microphone and smiled. She looked utterly beautiful in her soft-pink ballgown and sparkling crown. "I would like to expwess my sincere gwatitude to the people of Austwia for making this twip such a super success." She paused. "It has been a weally wemarkable week, full of adventure – and so I insist that we all welax and have a pleasuwable evening."

The band began to play and the audience, made up of some of the richest and most influential people in Europe, applauded. The clapping grew louder when the crown prince of Norway held out a hand to invite the princess onto the dance floor.

Blushing, Tiara removed her crown and placed it on her table. "Oh my!" she exclaimed. "I'll twy, but I'm not tewwibly good at the foxtwot."

At a table to the side of the room, Fangs Enigma leaned over to Puppy Brown. "Foxtrot," he said. "Is that in there?"

Puppy tapped a quick command into her laptop and hit "Enter". "It is now." She smiled. "Along with the waltz, the quickstep and the tango."

The secret agents watched the princess whirl around the room with her partner.

"Do you think it will work?" asked Fangs.

"It has to," Puppy replied. "Unless you want to go back to London and admit that we lost the princess and the Jade Panther in one go."

Fangs shuddered at the thought. "You've done a great job, I have to admit. If I didn't know that was really RALF…"

"No one will ever know it's RALF," said Puppy. "I've rewritten Cube's program so that it will stay looking like the princess permanently. I've even added artificial ageing software, so that she'll appear to grow older over time."

"What if Cube tries to deactivate the android from HQ?"

"I've changed the frequency in RALF's receiver," Puppy explained. "And, anyway, Cube thinks RALF was lost days ago. He'll be working on a replacement by now."

A shadow fell over the table. "One blood milkshake, an orange juice and a glass of the finest champagne this place has to offer," Issy Death said, putting the drinks down on the table. She sat and cuddled up to Fangs.

"Heard from your ex-boss?" the vampire asked, taking a sip of his drink.

Issy shook her head. "No, and I don't want to."

"He escaped," said Fangs matter-of-factly. "But he'll be back."

"Forget about him," Issy said, jumping to her feet. She grabbed Fangs's hand. "Dance with me."

"I'll give it a try," said Fangs, "but my specialty

is the *fang*-dango." Fangs scooped Issy up into his arms and carried her, giggling, to the dance floor.

Puppy laughed and settled back in her chair to watch them. Had she been looking the other way, she might have noticed a green-gloved hand appear from beneath the top table and take Princess Tiara's royal crown...

ABOUT THE AUTHOR

TOMMY DONBAVAND was born and brought up in
Liverpool and has worked at numerous careers
that have included clown, actor, theatre producer,
children's entertainer, drama teacher, storyteller
and writer. He is the author of the popular thirteen-
book series Scream Street. His other books include
Zombie!; *Wolf*; *Uniform*; and Doctor Who: *Shroud of
Sorrow*. His non-fiction books for children and their
parents, *Boredom Busters* and *Quick Fixes for Bored
Kids*, have helped him to become a regular guest
on radio stations around the UK and he also writes
for a number of magazines, including *Creative Steps*
and Scholastic's *Junior Education*.

Tommy lives in Lancashire with his family.
He is a huge fan of all things Doctor Who, plays blues
harmonica and makes a mean balloon poodle.
He sees sleep as a waste of good writing time.
You can find out more about Tommy and his books
at his website: www.tommydonbavand.com
Visit the Fangs website at: www.fangsvampirespy.co.uk

TEST YOUR SECRET-AGENT

Spot the Difference (There are eight to spot.)

SKILLS WITH THESE PUZZLES!

Royal Rescue Facts

How well do you know this book?
Answer these questions and find out!

1) What does the Jade Panther steal
in the opening scene of this book?

2) What is Phlem's secretary called?

3) What is Princess Tiara's secret identity?

UNLOCK THE SECRET MISSION FILES!

Want to gain access to highly classified MPI files?

Decode the word below and enter the answer at

WWW.FANGSVAMPIRESPY.CO.UK/MISSION3

Which Fangs character is this?

JNER DAPTHEA

- -